The Times They Used to Be

The Times They Used to Be

LUCILLE CLIFTON

illustrated by E. B. LEWIS

DELACORTE PRESS

Published by Delacorte Press
an imprint of Random House Children's Books
a division of Random House, Inc.
1540 Broadway, New York, New York 10036

Text copyright © 1974 by Lucille Clifton
Illustrations copyright © 2000 by Earl B. Lewis
Originally published by Holt, Rinehart and Winston 1974
First Delacorte Press Edition 2000

Visit us on the Web! www.randomhouse.com/teens
Educators and librarians, for a variety of teaching tools,
visit us at www.randomhouse.com/teachers

Library of Congress Cataloging-in-Publication Data

Clifton, Lucille.
   The times they used to be / by Lucille Clifton; illustrated by Earl B. Lewis.—1st
Delacorte Press ed.
      p. cm.
   Summary: A young black girl relates the adventures of the summer her Uncle Sunny died
and her best friend broke out in sin because she wasn't saved.
   ISBN 0-385-32126-0
   1. Afro-Americans—Juvenile fiction. [1. Afro-Americans—Fiction.] I. Lewis, Earl B., ill.
II. Title.

PZ7.C6224 Ti 2000
[Fic]—dc21   99-042411

The text of this book is set in 16-point Bernhard Modern.
Book design by Debora Smith
Manufactured in the United States of America
December 2000
10 9 8 7 6 5 4 3 2 1

For Kim, Karyn, and Mikah
Whose Mama Was There

—L.C.

To Rashida Watson, my soul mate

—E.B.L.

Mama, Mama,
tell us about when you was a girl.

Yeah, Mama,
tell us one of them stories
about the olden days.

Yeah, Mama,
we like to hear about the times they used to be.

Well,
I do seem to remember once, a while ago.
It wasn't these times. . . .

It is the story
of what happened to Tassie Scott
the time sin broke all out in her body
because she wasn't saved.
And also about me,
and how it was
the summer my uncle Sunny

followed the nun
back and forth
across the Grider Street bridge.

All us colored lived in Cold Spring
or else around William Street, downtown.
Our family was Cold Spring Colored
and everybody thought we was rich.
We lived in a big old duplex
right next to Tassie and her granny,
and Uncle Sunny, my mama's baby brother,
had a cottage in the rear.

He was tall and skinny,
but had Mama's color
and her smiling ways.
He got a check from the government
so he didn't have to work.
Daddy said he never had worked,
and one time Mama and him had a big fuss
    about it.
Oh, she was crazy about Uncle Sunny.

"He the smartest man in the world
next to your daddy!" she would smile.

He had been to Tuskegee
and then overseas with the 92d,
the all-colored division,
and he could see spirits and things
'cause he was born with a veil over his face.

Uncle Sunny come in our house
one early summer night hollering at Mama,
and waving his arms all around.
"Come with me,
come with me, Lil."
Daddy grabbed him by the shirt
and asked him what was the matter,
and Uncle Sunny told about how he was just
    driving around
and got to the Grider Street bridge
when he saw a nun
walking out in front of the car,
and how he speeded up
to offer her a ride.

When he got right up
to where he should of been next to her,
she looked over and smiled at the car
and disappeared into thin air.

Well, Mama was all ready to go with him
and see the nun-ghost for herself,
but Daddy wouldn't let her.
He said it was too late
for her to be going out,
and Sunny was most probably
just shell-shocked
from being in the war
with the 92d Division;
anyhow wasn't no such thing
as a nun-ghost.

Ended up she never did go,
but Uncle Sunny followed that nun all summer
back and forth across the bridge;
some nights going real fast
to catch her quick,
and some nights easing on up to her
before she knew he was there.
But every time,
soon as he was close,
she would turn around to smile at the car
and be gone,
just drop right out of the headlights.

"I'll catch her, though,"
he would say to us,
"and give her a lift in my car,
just like a man and a soldier."

That was the summer
my uncle Sunny drove after the nun
on the Grider Street bridge at night.
Satchel Paige was up to the majors
and Ralph Bunche was at the U.N.
The Elks' convention was coming to town.

I was twelve years old
and got my first pair of wedgies.
I wore a hat with a feather to church,
and my wedgies,
and fell flat on my behind.
And sin broke all out
in the body of my best friend.
It was 1948.

Mama was a riveter in an airplane factory during
    the war,
but when it was over she went back to folding at
    the laundry.

Daddy worked in the steel mill
with Granddaddy and Big Uncle,
and I just went to school.

I was in the eighth grade.
Twelve years old and in the eighth grade.
I was a good girl
and smart, too.
Tassie was thirteen
but in the same grade as me.

Me and Tassie.
Tassie and me.
We was best friends;
going to the show together, and hitching on the
    iceman's truck,
and going on long walks
over to the white folks' section
to look in their windows.
One time we walked all the way uptown
to see Johnny Ray come out of the radio station.
He touched Tassie's hand,
and she swore
she wasn't never going to write with it anymore
or nothing.

Her whole name was Tallahassie May Scott
and she lived next door to us with her granny.
And she wasn't saved.

One thing about Tassie
was that she hadn't never joined no church.
Everything else
she always did right
and never said a word,
but when Gran Scott fussed with her
about being saved,
Tassie would fuss right back.

"I just want to belong with my friends, Granny,"
she would beg.
"Just let me join Baptist."

"No, indeed,"
Gran Scott would say, shaking her head,
"you must be sanctified and made holy."

"Sanctified is too country, Granny."
Her granny would shake her head real slow
    and old.

"You thirteen years old now,
old enough to know sin.
Baptists shout on Sunday
and drunk on Monday.
Come to God
before your body is made all unclean."
And she would walk away mumbling.

Over on Purdy Street,
one thing we used to do
is sit on the curb by the bus stop evenings
to get first light
before we was supposed to go home.
Me and Tassie
would usually get there early
to trade comics or sing a little.
But this one night
I'm thinking about,
Tassie didn't want to read no books
and she didn't want to sing neither.

"Well, what is the matter, Tassie?"
I kept asking.

"Nothing."

"Well, how come you acting
like something is?"

"I said wasn't nothing wrong,
didn't I?"

"Shoot, go on then!"
And I walked away a little.

"Oh, come on now, Sooky,
don't be mad."

Tassie walked over to where I was,
all the big boys' eyes coming with her.
She was real light skinned
and had good hair
and I was proud to be best friends with her,
me and my nappy-headed self.

"Well, what's wrong then?"
I asked again.
Tassie slumped down to the curb
and I slumped too.

"Sooky, I got to run away."

"How come?"

"I got to go see my daddy."
Tassie's daddy was in Florida
on the chain gang.

"How come?"

"Well, I got a problem, Sooky,
and he the only one can help me."

"What kind a problem?"
Tassie didn't say nothing
for a long time.
When the lights came on
she jumped up and stood awhile
with her hands in her pockets.
"I done become a sinner,"
she whispered all of a sudden.
"I'm a unclean sinner
and my daddy is a sinner too,
and that's why he got to help me!"

And she ran on home.

Didn't even stop
to get first light
and neither did I.

When I got home
Uncle Sunny was over,
and everybody was sitting around the table
drinking cherry pop
and listening to him tell Mama
about the nun.

"I almost got right up on her
last night, Lil.
Seem like I just had to reach out my hand
and I could touch her,
but then all of a sudden
she was gone again."

"Sunny Jim, sweetheart,"
Mama said, smiling,
"how come you want to catch her so bad?"

"'Cause I'm a man, Lil."
He patted Mama's hand.

"I know about nuns.
I was over in Italy
in the war,
and Lil,
when the 92d Division
come rolling into town
all of us up on tanks
and wearing them uniforms,
all those Italian people
just went to shouting and waving at us,
so glad to see us,
and the nuns come running out
smiling at us
and brought us food
and everything.
They was good to us,
and I want to show
how I remember.
Payback, Lil,
payback,
just like any man."

Daddy went to turn on Amos and Andy.
"Hush now,
we got to hear."

Everybody fixed their chairs close to the radio
and I dropped down on the floor
next to it.

"Shell-shocked most probably,"
Daddy mumbled
as he sat back down in his chair.

We used to listen to *Stella Dallas*
and old Fibber and Molly
and *The Green Hornet*.
Me and Mama would wait up
to hear the Hit Parade,
and I would keep pencil and paper
to try and get down
the words of the number-one song.
But Amos and Andy was our favorite.
Uncle Sunny would come from the poolroom
in time to hear them every day.
In time to hear
Amos and Andy every day,
just like it was a job,
Daddy always said.

After the show was over
Uncle Sunny left for the bridge,
and Daddy said he was taking me
and Mama for a surprise.

"You get a sweater
and a stool,"
he grinned.

"Where we going, Daddy?"
I was real excited.

"Just you wait."

Me and Mama got the stool
and our sweaters
and Daddy took a dining-room chair
and we headed out.

"How come we going for a walk
with chairs and stuff, Daddy?"

"Just come on."

"What is this about, Richard?"
Mama asked.

Daddy looked at Mama
all nervous and smiley
and laughed.
"You'll see, Miss Lilly,
you'll see."

Close to the corner on Ferry Street
some people were standing
looking in the hardware-store window.
Daddy led us around
to the front of the crowd.

"All right now, all right,
I got my family here with me now."

People made room for him
to put down the chair
and the stool,
and we sat down,
Mama holding me in the chair.
I stared in the hardware window.

A radio was in it,
but a kind with a little window
where the knobs was supposed to be,
and in that window
was white people
dancing and singing plain as anything.

"Oh, Lord."
My mama held me real tight.
"Lord have mercy,
is they little movies, Richard?"

"They calling it
the television,"
Daddy whispered,
"and them white people is in New York City
just having a good time right now.
We ain't going to look too long;
a fellow was telling me
the tubes is poison."

"Oh, Lord," I whispered too.

That evening,
after we was all in bed,
some police come to the house and woke us up.
They said they had been looking for Mama.
They said Uncle Sunny had drove his car
off the Grider Street bridge—
and drowned.

Next day I told Tassie
I would run away with her.
We would have to wait
till after the Elks' convention
but I wanted to go too.

She was glad,
like I knew she would be.
She needed somebody like me
if she was ever going to find her daddy,
or Florida either;
and I wanted to find out something
about sin, too,
and about going to heaven
if you wasn't saved
but was a grown man
like Uncle Sunny.

We had to wait
till after the convention
because my mama always rented space
to out-of-town colored
when they came through,
and I figured she wouldn't feel so bad
about me being gone
if she made some money.
She would be glad to have
the extra money.
Anyhow,
I wanted to see the parade.
But after that,
we was on our way
to Florida.

"We ought to try
to get us something new
to wear."
Me and Tassie
was planning
on the front steps.

"How come?"
she asked me.

"Girl,
I guess we might have to pass
for fifteen or sixteen years old!
We need to get our hair done too."

"I just need mine rolled up."

"Mama do both of ours,"
I whispered,
peeking sideways at her straight bangs
and ponytail.

"She going to ask how come."

"For the Elks, girl,"
I laughed.
"We'll say we want it done
for the parade."

So that was that.

"How we going?" Tassie looked at me
and waited.
This was where being

on the honor roll
came in handy.

"You know I'll figure it out,"
I smiled,
"don't worry."

She smiled,
sure of me,
and started to hum.

"Tassie, how your daddy come
to be on the chain gang, anyhow?"

"He a sinner."

"I know,
but what kind of a sinner?"

"I don't know, Sooky,"
she said,
"I'm real new at sin."

And we both hummed
"With My Eyes Wide Open I'm Dreaming."

After a while
we walked over
to the bus stop
and sat on the curb
to wait for first light.

"Tassie,
how come you know
you a sinner now?"

"Sin done broke all out
in my body, Sooky."

"But how you know?"

"Just do, that's all."

"Did your granny tell you?"

"She don't even know it yet
herself."

"Well, how come you know
if she don't?"

"It's my body, ain't it?
That's why I got to
get to my daddy
and talk to him
before she finds out."

The lights switched on
and we ran for first light
and then for home.

Across the street from our house
all the windows were bright
and hands kept reaching for shades
to pull them up and down,
and up and down again.
We could hear Bobby Seek
in there screaming again.
He had been
in the 92d Division too.

Next day I cleaned up the kitchen
While *Let's Pretend* was on
and then started to wash the woodwork.

Every week
that old cracked-up woodwork
had to get washed.
Mama always said stuff like
"You can be clean if you raggedy."
But I had promised myself
I wasn't never having woodwork
when I grew up,
just smooth wall
right down to the floor.
Around eleven,
Rudy, the number man, stopped by,
and him and Daddy was talking
about what happened.
I finished up the woodwork in one room
and sneaked my sweater off the hook
in the room where Mama was resting
and went over to Tassie's.

"When's the funeral?"
she wanted to know.

"Tomorrow."

"Who's got the body?"

"Meadows."

"Let's go view it."

"Okay."

We whispered the whole thing.

Meadows Funeral Home
was just a few blocks away,
right across from the church,
and we used to view the bodies
whenever new ones came in.
We would ask Duval Meadows
if his daddy had any new folks
and whenever he said yeah,
we would walk over and view.
One time we had gone over
and it was a girl
in the coffin,
looked like she wasn't
no older than us.

We had run scared
out of there
and all the way
to Tassie's.
Gran Scott had laughed
to see us come
flying in the house.

"They's short graves too,
you better get right.
They's short graves too!"
We hadn't never thought about it before
and it really got us.

Uncle Sunny lay long
in his soldier's suit.
Me and Tassie took seats
in the middle of the mourners' row
and watched him.
We sat for a long time,
quiet,
full of Uncle Sunny
and pictures of Jesus
staring at us from the walls.

"Wonder what is he thinking about,"
Tassie finally whispered.
"Nothing. He's dead."

"I mean Jesus."

"I imagine he's in heaven
talking with the prophets and things."

"Bet he's talking to your uncle Sunny, too!"

I glanced at her.

"No he ain't!"
I spoke even softer.
"Uncle Sunny ain't even in heaven.
Tassie, he wasn't saved."

Tassie started shivering all over.

"How you know he wasn't, Sooky?"

"'Cause I heard my daddy say it.
Uncle Sunny never did join no church
and he's gone to flaming hell for sure."

"Oh, Lord." Tassie was shivering more.

"What's the matter with you, Tassie?"
She was shaking so hard
she was bumping me.

"Was that why he was trying so hard
to catch the nun?"

"I don't know.
Mama say she just hopes
he caught up with her
at the last
so she could bless him
and he wouldn't have to die in sin."

Tassie jumped up
and covered up her face with her hands
and just started moaning and shaking all over.
She went and ran up
and fell down across the body
crying, "Bless me, bless me," to Uncle Sunny.
And I jumped up
and hollered
and ran out of there too,

crying and running
right out into the street.
'Cause it looked like they was a cross
writ right on the back of Tassie's dungarees—
in blood.
Sin!

I run right into Mama.
Her and Reverend Littlejohn was standing on
    the steps
that led up to the church
where the skating club used to be.
When she saw me light out of the home
she come across to meet me.

"Sylvia, what's the matter, baby?"
Mama grabbed me by the arms
to keep me from falling down.

"Mama, Mama, sin done broke all out of
    Tassie's body
in blood
and she's having a fit
in front of Jesus."

Reverend Littlejohn rubbed his head
where it was bald.

"Where is she, child?"

"Viewing the body," I sobbed.
"Uncle Sunny gone and now Tassie gone die too."

"Hush up, Sylvia."
Mama let go my arms and headed into Meadows.

Tassie was laying on the floor
in front of the coffin
with her eyes closed
and her arms crossed,
crying and rocking herself.
Mama pulled her up
and sat holding Tassie on her lap.

"Don't, Mama," I hollered,
"Jesus done marked her on her pants!"

Mama shifted Tassie's body
and saw the stain.

It had got bigger
and looked like a hand spread out.
Reverend Littlejohn,
standing at the doorway,
saw it and shook his head
and grinned and walked on out.
Mama smiled.
Then she pulled old crying Tassie close to her
and walked both of us to the coffin.

"Oh, Sunny Jim," she whispered,
still smiling,
"it's a sign all right.
Let's go home, Sylvia.
Life keeps on, you know."

She stood Tassie up
and wiped her face with her dress hem.
"Hush up, Tallahassie,
ain't nothing wrong with you."
Then Mama wrapped her kerchief
round Tassie's pants,
and we all walked home.

My mama give me and Tassie a Kool-Aid
and told us about coming into your nature,
and about how we must stay good girls
and we would be fine
and not go to hell.
She took Tassie to her granny
and fussed with Gran Scott 'bout sin talk
and told her to explain to Tassie
how to take care of herself instead;
and then she explained it to me.
I was so tired I went to bed early
with next day being Uncle Sunny's funeral
       and all.

Just before I got to sleep
I heard on the radio
that President Truman had stopped Jim Crow
       in the army.

The 92d was gone.